THE
TOTALLY NINJA
RACCOONS
AND THE
SECRET OF
NESSMUK LAKE

by Kevin Coolidge

Illustrated by Jubal Lee

Be a reading ninja!

Kevin Coolidge

The Totally Ninja Raccoons Are:

Rascal:
He's the shortest brother and loves doughnuts. He's great with his paws and makes really cool gadgets. He's a little goofy and loves both his brothers, even when they pick on him, but maybe not right then.

Bandit:
He's the oldest brother. He's tall and lean. He's super smart and loves to read. He leads the Totally Ninja Raccoons, but he couldn't do it by himself.

Kevin:
He may be the middle brother, but he refuses to be stuck in the middle. He has the moves and the street smarts that the Totally Ninja Raccoons are going to need, even if it does sometimes get them into trouble as well as out of trouble.

CONTENTS

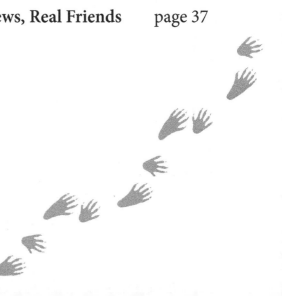

Scotty pulls out a greenish, purplish egg that shimmers in the sunlight.

GYPSY HATCHES A PLAN

It's summer in Wellsboro, Pennsylvania. The sky is blue with white, puffy clouds. The sun shines onto a neatly trimmed lawn. It's a beautiful day for a picnic, and a nap, especially if you are a cat.

There's a freshly, painted picnic table with a clowder of cats. A group of cats is called a clowder or a clutter. Sometimes, it's called a glaring. That's because of Gypsy the Cat, founder of the Cat Board.

Gypsy, a rather plump calico, glares at the gathering of the Cat Board. Have you heard of the Cat Board? It's the shadowy organization entirely made up of felines who plan on taking over the world. Well, as soon as they get in just one more nap, and maybe some tasty Tuna Yum Yums.

"This super-secret meeting will now come to order," yowls Gypsy.

A nearly furless cat clears her throat, and speaks up, "Why are we having this private meeting out in the open, and out in the sunshine? I could get a sunburn!"

Gypsy looks uncomfortable. "Uh, my hidden lair is having some work done," she meows.

A large, silky Persian cat puts her nose in the air. "It smells," sniffs the Persian.

"It just needs a little spring cleaning," meows Gypsy.

A large Siamese cat smirks, "It's summer, and the smell is because of those darn Totally Ninja Raccoons, and their stink bombs. I can smell it from here!"

A slim black and white cat perks up. He looks like he is wearing a little tuxedo. It's Huck! "That smell is Finn's butt. He farted!" laughs Huck.

An all black cat licks his lips. "I had some Tuna Yum Yums for lunch. Soooo good," purrs Finn.

Gypsy the cat raises her voice, "Speaking of those pesky Ninja Raccoons, I have a simply brilliant idea to get rid of them. It's the best idea."

"You've meowed that before," says the Siamese Cat.

"It's a great plan, a fool-proof plan. Ok, fellow felines of the Cat Board, I'd like to introduce Scotty, a visiting member, all the way from Scotland," announces Gypsy.

A big, bulky Scottish Fold sits up and speaks, "Awrite, members of the moggie board, ahm here tae introduce th' plan tae eliminate th' pure ninja raccoons," burrs Scotty.

"What did he say?" asks the Persian.

"Could you please speak American?" says Gypsy.

"Sorry, meaty moggie, Ah'll spick nice an' slaw fur ye. Ahhuv have the answer to all yer troubles," says Scotty. He pulls out a greenish, purplish egg that shimmers in the sunlight.

"Why, it's an egg!" exclaims the Persian Cat.

"I love eggs! I'll take mine scrambled," shouts Huck.

"How is an egg going to take care of the Ninja Raccoons?" sniffs the Siamese Cat.

"It's no the egg, mind ye, but what wull emerge from the egg," says Scotty.

"I'd like my egg fried please, and a side of scrapple," says Finn as he licks his lips.

3

"No eggs, omelets, or mystery meats. Now, what is Scotland known for?" asks Gypsy.

"Bacon?" asks Finn.

"Kilts and castles?" asks the Persian.

"Bagpipes?" asks the Siamese.

"Bacon!" shouts Finn.

"Nah, lads an' lassies, we have Nessie, the famous monster of Loch Ness, and this is one of hur eggs," says Scotty proudly.

Gypsy looks excited and rubs her paws together, "We place the egg in our local Lake Nessmuk, and when the egg hatches, our "Nessie" will totally take care of the Ninja Raccoons, and I will be as well-known as Scotland. I mean--the Cat Board will become famous," corrects Gypsy.

"It just might work," says the Sphinx.

"It's brilliant!' shouts Gypsy.

"Cheers," says Scotty.

"Will we be getting unicorns? I love unicorns! It's the national animal of Scotland," chirps Huck.

"But when do we get scrapple?" asks Finn.

"I could go fur some haggis," says Scotty.

"Haggis? What's that?" asks Finn.

"A fine Scottish puddin' served in a sheep's tummy," says Scotty.

"Uggh, that would make Finn fart!" yelps Huck.

"Everything makes Finn fart!" yell the other members of the Cat Board.

"No unicorns, haggis, or foul odors, but we'll be hatching Nessie's egg, and it will soon be the end of those pesky raccoons," says Gypsy.

"It better be, Gypsy. It better be," scowls the Siamese.

"It will be. It will be," promises Gypsy. As she waddles off to her concealed hideout, the members of the Cat Board quietly point and laugh at the red paint stain smeared across her butt.

"Hey, did anyone check and see if this picnic table was dry before we sat down?" asks the Sphinx.

"It's time for Rascal to continue his swimming lessons,"
says Bandit.

2

SOMETHING IS FISHY

The Totally Ninja Raccoons are visiting Lake Nessmuk, just outside Wellsboro. Kevin twirls his broomstick staff. Bandit wades into the water, and Rascal rests on the bank with "Pinkie," the flamingo inner-tube, around his waist.

"It's time for Rascal to continue his swimming lessons," says Bandit.

"I've already been in the deep end at the Packer Park pool," answers Rascal.

"Aww, that doesn't count. You never took off your floatie," says Kevin.

"I didn't want Pinkie to get lonely, and it was dark and deep. I didn't know what was in there," pouts Rascal.

"It was the town pool. There wasn't anything lurking except maybe some leaves," says Bandit.

7

"You don't know! There could have been a sea monster," says Rascal.

"There's no such thing as sea monsters," says Kevin

"You said that about Bigfoot, and werewolves, and...," says Rascal.

"Wellsboro, Pennsylvania is a long way from the ocean," says Kevin.

"There have been reptilian creatures spotted in the Finger Lake region of New York State. That's only a short flight from Tioga County for our friend the thunderbird," says Bandit.

"And you said Krampus wasn't real, and he brought me a brand new baseball glove," says Rascal.

"Well, Billy the Werewolf did slobber all over yours," says Kevin.

"Water does cover approximately 71% of the Earth, and it has always hidden secrets in its depths." Bandit claps his paws together. "Now, let's get Rascal into Lake Nessmuk and teach him to swim," says Bandit.

"Uh, wait a minute. It's dark and deep, and I can't see anything. What if there's a sea monster in there?" asks Rascal.

"Nessmuk Lake is too small for a sea monster. We need to continue our ninja training, and you still can't swim," says Bandit.

"Aww, alright, but I'm taking Pinkie with me," says Rascal.

Rascal slowly shuffles up to the water's edge and puts his little black paw into the water.

"Brrrr, it's cold!" shouts Rascal.

"It's early summer, and the water can still be cold, but you do have fur, you know," replies Bandit.

"Summer! Now all I need is a cold birch beer. Why can't we do this when it's warm and sunny out?" asks Rascal.

"Because 1. We are nocturnal and 2. People would see us," says Kevin.

"There are people here now. There's a boat over there," says Rascal.

Bandit ducks down. "Be quiet everyone, and stop playing with your staff, Kevin," whispers Bandit.

"Fine, but I don't know how I'm going to become a better ninja without practice," whispers Kevin.

"Where's Rascal?" asks Bandit.

"He's drifting out into the middle of the lake," replies Kevin.

Rascal floats out into the lake. He lays on his back with his paws lazily trailing in the water. He suddenly sits up and yelps, "Something just brushed my leg! It's a sea monster!"

"There's no such thing as sea monsters," quips Kevin.

The water ripples a short distance from Rascal. A spout of water erupts from the lake's surface. The nearby boat overturns, and the men fall into the lake, splashing and making a lot of noise.

Rascal feels the waves and hears the noise. He starts paddling to shore as fast as he can.

"Wow, Rascal is really moving fast!" shouts Kevin.

"He's doing it! He's learning to swim!" shouts Bandit.

"He still has Pinkie on, though," says Kevin.

Rascal hits the shore and keeps running, "It's behind me! I'm--*pant, pant*--I want to go back to the clubhouse."

"Hmmm, those ripples do seem pretty big for a fish," says Bandit.

"There are some pretty big Walleyes in this lake," says Kevin.

"It must have been a fish. There's no such thing as sea monsters. Let's go back to the clubhouse. I need to read about what kind of fish could do that," says Bandit.

"And I'm hungry," says Kevin.

Kevin and Bandit turn from the lake and start heading back to the clubhouse. Rascal is way ahead of them with a deflated Pinkie flopping around his waist.

"Rascal sure is moving fast for a raccoon with such little legs. I hope he doesn't drink all the birch beer before I get there," says Kevin.

"Teaching Rascal to swim sure made me hungry."

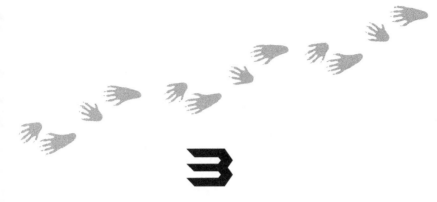

3

SECRET OF THE LAKE

The Totally Ninja Raccoons recover from their adventures in their clubhouse tucked into a corner of the junkyard. Bandit reads a book about ichthyology. You know, fish. Rascal tinkers with his newest invention, a camera, and Kevin makes a peanut butter sandwich with extra strawberry jam.

Kevin takes a huge bite of the sandwich and says with his mouth full, "Teaching Rascal to swim sure made me hungry."

"You didn't do anything except watch me almost get eaten by a sea monster, and don't talk with your mouth full," says Rascal.

"Bah, there's no such thing as sea monsters. Besides, Nessmuk is only a lake. It's much too small for a sea monster," answers Kevin.

"I'm reading *Fish of the World*, and there are fish large enough to have upset that boat," says Bandit.

"So, you think it was a fish?" asks Rascal.

"No, there aren't any fish native to Pennsylvania waters large enough to do that," says Bandit.

"See, it's a monster, a sea monster," says Rascal.

"Maybe it was a snapping turtle? There's no such thing as sea monsters," says Kevin.

Bandit pulls a green, dusty book off the shelf and leafs through it, "According to *The Secret of Loch Ness*, there is a sea monster in a lake in Scotland."

"We're over a hundred miles from Scotland," says Kevin.

"No, not Scotland, Pennsylvania! Scotland, the country in Europe," says Bandit.

"But Lake Nessmuk is right here in Wellsboro," says Rascal.

"There's no such thing as sea monsters," says Kevin.

"Scotland's lake monster is known by the name of Nessie, and some scientists think it could be a dinosaur," says Bandit.

"Nah, dinosaurs are all extinct. That means they are long gone," says Kevin.

"There could be a Nessie right here in Wellsboro!" shouts Rascal.

"But sea monsters and Nessie don't exist, and dinosaurs are gone," replies Kevin.

"Physical proof of the creature would be helpful in proving its existence," says Bandit, rubbing his little black paws on his furry chin.

"I'm working on my new camera that can take photos in complete darkness. I'm calling it the Cat's Eye," says Rascal.

"Cool name, but the Cat Board won't like that. Hey, we could sell the photo for a lot of money and be famous!" shouts Kevin.

"I could buy all the birch beer I could drink," says Rascal.

"General Tso's chicken every night, AND pork-fried rice with all the pork still in it, yum," says Kevin as he smacks his lips.

"I wouldn't get too excited. There have been photos taken of the creature before, but it's never been proven they are real," says Bandit.

"The editor of the Wellsboro Gazette wants to sell papers. He doesn't care if it's real. Let's go!" shouts Kevin.

"I am curious to confirm the existence of a thought-to-be extinct dinosaur," says Bandit.

"I need to test my new camera, and earn money for birch beer and a new screwdriver," says Rascal.

"We can do this, guys, because we are..." asks Bandit.

"Going to get rich?" asks Kevin.

"Going to see a dinosaur?" asks Rascal.

"Awww, come on guys, we're the..." says Bandit.

"Totally Ninja Raccoons!' shout Kevin and Bandit together.

The Totally Ninja Raccoons grab their backpacks and run out the door. Rascal runs back in and grabs his camera off the table and stuffs it in the pack. "I still haven't figured out why photos turn out square when camera lenses are round..."

17

"Why, it's a wee unicorn!" exclaims Scotty.

4

GYPSY'S PLAN GETS SCRAMBLED

Gypsy feels grumpy. She sits on her desk in her hidden, but not quite as secret as she would like, cave. Her butt itches from the dried paint, and she can't quite reach it, and she has to talk to that Scottish Fold. His accent can be so hard to understand.

"So, have you planted the egg in Lake Nessmuk as we discussed? What was your name again?" meows Gypsy.

"Ye kin caw me Scotty, ye pie-eater moggie. Ah cannae place the egg. Thare's awready a beastie in thare," says Scotty.

"What? There's already a lake monster in Nessmuk? Well, put the egg in anyway. Two is twice as good as one," says Gypsy.

Scotty just shakes his head and his little ears flop over, "Th' loch is tae wee fur twa monsters, ye dumb moggie."

"Why do you keep calling me 'moggie'?" asks Gypsy.

"Tis whit we caw cats in bonnie Scotland," says Scotty.

"Err, right. Jolly good then, Scotty. Well, I'll just be getting my money back then," says Gypsy.

"You have not paid me yit, and a'hm from Scotland, nae Englan," snarls Scotty.

There's a loud cracking sound and a large *PoP*. "You better not get yolk on my floor. I just had this cave cleaned," complains Gypsy.

"Th' egg, it hus hatched!" exclaims Scotty.

"Egg shells all over my clean floor!" shouts Gypsy.

"Why, it's a wee unicorn!" exclaims Scotty.

"A unicorn! Unicorns are real?" asks Gypsy.

"The unicorn is the national animal of Scotlan' We coudna dae that if unicorns wurnae real," says Scotty.

"It was supposed to be an egg from the Loch Ness Monster! I paid for the Loch Ness Monster!" shouts Gypsy.

"Ye huvnae paid me yit. Tis easy tae git the' eggs messed up. Yin is greenish-purplish, 'n' the ither is purplish-greenish," explains Scotty.

"Unicorns can't come from eggs!" snorts Gyspy.

"Ken a lot aboot unicorns, daes ye?" asks Scotty.

"Don't let it track up my clean floor!" says Gypsy.

"A unicorn daes whit it wants," explains Scotty.

"Not in my super-secret, clean cave, it doesn't!" yowls Gypsy.

The unicorn scoots between Scotty's legs and disappears. "The unicorn's run off intae th' woods," Scotty announces.

"Good, mah floor wull bade wash, or efter ye pick up the eggshells. Ack! Now you have me doing it!" screams Gypsy.

"Ah will be gaun back tae Scoatlan'. Ah'll send a bill fur th' unicorn," explains Scotty.

"Naw, ahm not paying fur a unicorn. Aggggh! Darn you, Scotty!" yowls Gypsy.

"We have to be quiet if we are going to sneak up on this lake monster," says Bandit.

5

CREATURE FEATURE

It's a dark night with just a little moonlight shimmering on the surface of the lake. The Totally Ninja Raccoons quietly make their way around the edges of Nessmuk. Bandit leads, then Kevin, and Rascal lags behind in the rear.

"I can't wait to test my special lens for my camera, and get a photo of the Lake Nessmuk Monster. I wonder if I can get the monster to smile?" asks Rascal.

"I can't wait until we get paid," says Kevin.

"What are you going to spend your money on, Bandit?" asks Rascal.

"Shhh, this is the perfect opportunity to practice our ninja stealth," whispers Bandit.

"How do you get a photo of a lake monster," whispers Kevin.

"With my special camera lens. I told you all about it. Don't you remember?" asks Rascal.

"It's a joke," whispers Kevin.

"No, your attempt at stealth is a joke," whispers Bandit.

"Oh, okay: What is the punch line to your silly joke?" asks Rascal.

"Unique up on him," chuckles Kevin. "How do you catch a tame lake monster?"

"How?" asks Bandit.

"Tame way… unique up on them," laughs Kevin.

"I don't get it?" says Rascal.

"He's trying to be clever, and using the word 'unique' as a homophone for 'you sneak' explains Bandit.

"Oh, I don't take photos with a phone. I find I get much better quality with my camera," says Rascal.

"A homophone is a word that sounds the same as another word but has a different meaning or spelling. 'Flower' and 'flour' are homophones because they are pronounced the same, but you can't bake doughnuts using daisies," explains Bandit.

Rascal smacks his lips, "I love doughnuts!"

"We know!" exclaim Kevin and Bandit.

"The joke was funnier before you had to explain it," pouts Kevin.

"We have to be quiet if we are going to sneak up on this lake monster," says Bandit.

The raccoons get really still and really quiet and start quietly walking around the lake.

"I think I see something!" yells Rascal.

"It's the lake monster! We are going to be rich!" shouts Kevin.

"Take several photos, and let's see if we can't get closer, and quieter," whispers Bandit.

A deep voice comes from behind the raccoons, "I'd make sure to take the lens cap off."

The Ninja Raccoons are startled and yell, "Ahhhh, what was that!"

Make it a good photo, but not too good.
The whole idea is to let people think it's fake."

6

THE LAKE EFFECT

The Ninja Raccoons are totally surprised. Kevin quickly spins around with his staff. Bandit turns and looks down, and Rascal checks his camera.

"What is that?" shouts Kevin.

"My observation is that it is the creature of Nessmuk Lake," says Bandit.

"I'm pretty sure the lens cap is already off," says Rascal.

A small, reptilian creature with really large flippers, a long neck, and a long tail looks from Kevin to Rascal to Bandit. "You aren't going to hit me with that, are you?" asks, lake creature looking at Kevin's staff.

"No, that's Kevin, he just likes to crack jokes and carry a big stick," says Bandit.

"It's a staff," says Kevin.

"A bo staff to be exact, and just what are you, other than the small, reptilian creature you appear to be?" asks Bandit.

"I'm Nessie, and I live in Nessmuk Lake," says Nessie.

"See, I have confirmed that it is indeed the lake creature," says Bandit.

"I thought a lake monster would be...bigger," says Kevin.

"I'm NOT a monster," says Nessie.

Rascal fiddles around with his camera, and a big flash goes off. "I knew the lens cap was off. The flash can't go off with the lens cap on," says Rascal.

The small, reptilian creature that calls itself Nessie looks shocked. "You didn't take my photo, did you?"

"Oh, it's why we're here. We are going to sell the photo and get rich!" says Kevin.

"I'm going to buy a whole case of birch beer, and more tools," says Rascal.

"I am looking forward to buying more books for my bookshelf," says Bandit.

Nessie looks upset. "It's rude to take a photo of someone without asking," says Nessie.

"How are we going to get rich, then?" asks Kevin.

"We could take a photo of our friend, Bigfoot?" says Rascal.

"Those always turn out blurry," says Bandit.

"If you publish a photo of your friend Bigfoot or me, then people will find out about us and never leave us alone. We'd have no privacy," says Nessie.

Bandit looks thoughtful, "Hmmm, I suppose that is true. The Totally Ninja Raccoons would hate for everyone to learn the location of our junkyard clubhouse," says Bandit.

"We know the location of Gypsy's super-secret lair. I even have a map," says Rascal.

"That doesn't count. No one wants to go there, and it smells," says Kevin.

"Those were my best stink bombs yet!" says Rascal proudly.

"If we don't turn in a photo, how are we going to get paid?" asks Kevin.

"There's a famous photo of my cousin in Scotland that most people think is a fake," says Nessie.

"That's it! We'll take a real photo, but we'll make it blurry so people will have to guess if it is real or not," says Bandit.

"There's not a lot of money in fake news, is there?" asks Kevin.

"Nessie is our new friend, and we don't want to give away her secrets," says Rascal.

"No, having a new friend is more important... I guess," says Kevin.

"Okay, Nessie, you get over there with that log, and Kevin, nail that reflector to it. People will wonder if it's a glowing eye, or just a highway reflector," says Bandit.

"Okay, but make sure to get my good side," says Nessie.

"Rascal, make it a good photo, but not too good. The whole idea is to let people come to the conclusion that it is a fake," says Bandit.

"I know. I know. I'll keep it just out of focus," says Rascal.

"I appreciate this, Ninja Raccoons. If there is anything I can ever do for you, just let me know," says Nessie.

"Well, you could try to teach Rascal to swim," says Kevin.

"It has been a bit of a challenge to teach him to swim," says Bandit.

"I'm a great swimmer. I could totally do that," says Nessie.

"Could I bring Pinkie?" asks Rascal.

"Of course," says Nessie.

"Now, let's get that photo taken so we can turn it in and get paid, because we are..."

"The Totally Ninja Raccoons," shout the raccoons.

"And Nessie too!" shouts Nessie.

*"Hello, this is Gypsy, head of the Cat Board.
Meow can you help me?"*

7

THE UNICORN PROBLEM

Gypsy shakes glitter off her paws and sniffs the air, "I don't know how all this glitter got in here, but at least my not-quite-so-secret lair smells great. It smells of breezy spring meadows, and summer sunshine."

Gypsy looks under her desk. "Now, where are my special Tuna Yum Yums?"

Gypsy sees a crumpled bag back in a corner and waddles over to it, "It's empty! It looks like a mouse chewed it open! A mouse in my house! I'd better have someone look into that," yowls Gypsy.

Gypsy jumps on to her desk with the big, red button that doesn't do anything anymore because of those pesky Ninja Raccoons. She's just about to take a little snooze when the phone rings.

"Hello, this is Gypsy, head of the Cat Board. Meow can you help me?" meows Gypsy.

"Hello, ye fat moggie," says Scotty.

"Ohhh, hello, Scotty. What do you want? Say, what's the natural predator of a mouse?" asks Gypsy.

"How come? Tis a wolf. A' body kens that," says Scotty

"Sure, sure, I knew that. I'll have to have Huck and Finn look into purchasing a wolf," says Gypsy.

"How come dae ye ask?" asks Scotty.

"I found my Tuna Yum Yums all eaten," says Gypsy

"Ye dinnae have a moose problem. You hae a unicorn dilemma. Unicorns love Tuna Yum Yums. Ah cuid tell ye how tae git rid of the unicorn, fur a cost," says Scotty.

"I'm NOT paying for your unicorn mistake," yowls Gypsy.

"Och, ye wull pay," chuckles Scotty.

"Nope, everything is fine, except for my bag of Tuna Yum Yums. In fact, my cave has never smelled fresher, and except for a little glitter, it's great!" chirps Gypsy.

"Is th' glitter a' th' colors o' th' rainbow?" asks Scotty.

"It's like a rainbow exploded in here!" exclaims Gypsy.

"Does yer cave reek o' spring meadows 'n' summer sunshine?" asks Scotty.

"It's delightful!" purrs Gypsy.

"Aye, ye hae a unicorn infestation. Th' glitter is unicorn scat, 'n' th' fresh wash scent is unicorn flatulence," says Scotty.

"I don't know what you are talking about," says Gypsy.

"Unicorn jobby 'n' farts, ye daft moggie," laughs Scotty.

"Noooo! Not unicorn poop! You have to catch this unicorn for me!" shouts Gypsy.

"Na yin ever catches a unicorn," burrs Scotty.

"The editor claims the photo is evidence --
evidence of a hoax!

8

FAKE NEWS,
REAL FRIENDS

The Totally Ninja Raccoons gather at Nessmuk Lake. Kevin is once again spinning his staff. Bandit is reading the paper, and Rascal is standing next to the water with Pinkie around his waist.

Bandit looks up from the paper. "Are you ready to continue your swimming lesson?" asks Bandit.

"I am. I have Pinkie blown up all the way again," replies Rascal.

"I think maybe we should just throw you right in and see if you sink or swim," says Kevin.

The water ripples and Nessie's head pops up. "I'm here to help you learn to swim," says Nessie.

"We aren't going out where it's deep, are we?" asks Rascal.

"Once you learn how to swim, how deep the water is doesn't matter. Don't worry. I won't let you sink. I'll be swimming underneath you and holding you up while you learn to use your arms and legs to swim through the water," says Nessie.

Rascal takes off Pinkie with great hesitancy and wades into the water. Bandit continues to read the paper. "Hey, Rascal, your photo is on page eleven," says Bandit.

"How does it look?" asks Rascal, as he walks deeper into the lake without even realizing it.

"It looks pretty grainy, and the only thing that really stands out is the red reflector. Nessie is in shadow," says Bandit.

"I was going for something artistic," says Rascal.

"How do I look? Do I look bigger?" asks Nessie.

"So, when are we getting our money?" asks Kevin.

"The editor claims the photo is evidence--evidence of a hoax! He writes that people will try anything to defame journalism, and that the photographer should be ashamed for trying to scare the public. It's perfectly safe to swim in Nessmuk Lake," says Bandit.

"It is perfectly safe to swim Nessmuk Lake. I'm swimming. I'm swimming!" shouts Rascal.

"He's swimming. Rascal is totally swimming," shouts Kevin.

"Of course he is, because we are..." says Bandit.

"The Totally Ninja Raccoons!" shout the three ninja brothers.

"And Nessie too!" shouts Nessie.

THE END

What is a Scottish Fold?

The Scottish Fold is a special breed of cat. They have a unique folded ear that makes them easy to spot. The Scottish fold is a blend of other breeds: The British and American shorthairs.

The first Scottish Fold was found on a farm in Scotland in 1961. Her name was Susie. She had white fur. A man named William Ross adopted one of her kittens, and named it Snooks. The kitten also shared the folded ear trait.

Snooks had kittens, and the trait proved dominant. Her kittens were born with folded ears. These kittens were called lop-eared cats, but later named Scottish Folds for the country they came from, Scotland.

About The Loch Ness Monster

Loch Ness is the second largest loch (lake) in Scotland with depths reaching over 750 feet! Loch Ness is famous for its creature, known as Nessie. The first recorded sighting was almost 1500 years ago!

In 1933, a man claimed the monster crossed the road in front of him. This led to increased interest in Nessie. Nessie hunters have used underwater cameras, fishing nets, and even submarines to try to locate her.

Some scientists think a family of sea dinosaurs, called plesiosaurs, might have become trapped in the loch. Other theories suggest the monster is a huge fish, surfacing trees, earthquake activity, or even swimming elephants.

Nessie is the most famous lake monster in the world. She's been in books, movies and TV shows. There's even a Loch Ness Monster roller coaster.Is the Loch Ness Monster real? Become a reading ninja, and decide for yourself.

About Unicorns

A unicorn is a
horse-like creature
with a single horn growing from its forehead. The horn is
usually long and straight, and unicorns have cloven hooves
like a cow, or a goat. Unicorn mean 'one horn'.

Unicorns are thought to be magical. The blood and tears
of a unicorn have healing properties, and the powder of a
unicorn horn is an cure for poison.

Unicorns are difficult to catch. Some myths says unicorns
can only be tamed by young maidens. The unicorn is the
natural enemy of the lion. Unicorns are mentioned in the
Bible nine times.

Unicorns are symbols of freedom, power and speed. The
unicorn is the national animal of Scotland. Some famous
people have claimed to see a unicorn. Are unicorns real?
Become a reading ninja, and decide for yourself.

About the Author

Kevin resides in Wellsboro, just a short hike from the Pennsylvania Grand Canyon. When he's not writing, you can find him at *From My Shelf Books & Gifts*, an independent bookstore he runs with his lovely wife, several helpful employees, and two friendly cats, Huck & Finn.

He's recently become an honorary member of the Cat Board, and when he's not scooping the litter box, or feeding Gypsy her tuna, he's writing more stories about the Totally Ninja Raccoons. Be sure to catch their next big adventure, *The Totally Ninja Raccoons Meet the Little Green Men*.

You can write him at:

From My Shelf Books & Gifts
7 East Ave., Suite 101
Wellsboro, PA 16901

www.wellsborobookstore.com

About the Illustrator

Jubal Lee is a former Wellsboro resident who now resides in sunny Florida, due to his extreme allergic reaction to cold weather.

He is an eclectic artist who, when not drawing raccoons, thunderbirds, and the like, enjoys writing, bicycling, and short walks on the beach.

CPSIA information can be obtained
at www.ICGtesting.com
Printed in the USA
LVHW051512060720
659897LV00005B/915

 9 781640 070967